Francesca Simon

HORRiD HENRY'S Royal Riot

Illustrated by Tony Ross

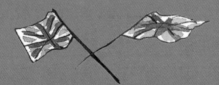

Orion
Children's Books

This collection first published in Great Britain in 2013
by Orion Children's Books
This paperback edition first published in 2014
by Orion Children's Books
a division of the Orion Publishing Group Ltd
Orion House
5 Upper St Martin's Lane
London WC2H 9EA
An Hachette UK Company

1 3 5 7 9 10 8 6 4 2

The Orion Publishing Group's policy is to use papers that are natural,
renewable and recyclable products and made from wood grown in
sustainable forests. The logging and manufacturing processes
are expected to conform to the environmental regulations of
the country of origin.

A catalogue record for this book is available from the British Library.

ISBN 978 1 4440 1196 8

Printed in China

www.orionbooks.co.uk
www.horridhenry.co.uk

Contents

HORRiD HENRY'S
Thank You Letter

Contents

For Sabrina and Jordan Jade

Chapter 1

Ahh! This was the life!
A sofa, a telly, a bag of crisps.
Horrid Henry sighed happily.

"Henry!" shouted Mum from the kitchen. "Are you watching TV?"

Henry blocked his ears.
Nothing was going to interrupt
his new favourite TV programme,
Terminator Gladiator.

"Answer me, Henry!" shouted Mum.
"Have you written your Christmas
thank you letters?"

bellowed
Henry.

Why not?

screamed
Mum.

"Because I haven't," said Henry.
"I'm busy." Couldn't she leave him
alone for two seconds?

Mum marched into the room and
switched off the TV.
"Hey!" said Henry. "I'm watching
Terminator Gladiator."

"Too bad," said Mum. "I told you,
no TV until you've written your
thank you letters."

"It's not fair!" wailed Henry.

"I've written all *my* thank you
letters," said Perfect Peter.

"Well done, Peter," said Mum.
"Thank goodness *one* of my children
has good manners."

Peter smiled modestly. "I always
write mine the moment I unwrap a
present. I'm a good boy, aren't I?"

"The best," said Mum.

"Oh, shut up, Peter," snarled Henry.

"Mum! Henry told me to shut up!"
said Peter.

"Stop being horrid, Henry. You will
write to Aunt Ruby, Great-Aunt
Greta and Grandma now."

"Now?" moaned Henry.
"Can't I do it later?"

"When's later?" said Dad.

"Later!" said Henry. Why wouldn't they stop nagging him about those stupid letters?

Chapter 2

Horrid Henry hated writing
thank you letters.

Why should he waste his precious
time saying thank you for presents?
Time he could be spending
reading comics, or watching TV.

But no.

He would barely unwrap a present
before Mum started nagging.

She even expected him to write to
Great-Aunt Greta and thank her for
the Baby Poopie Pants doll.

Great-Aunt Greta for one did not
deserve a thank you letter.

This year Aunt Ruby had sent him
a hideous lime green cardigan.
Why should he thank her for that?

True, Grandma had given him £15,
which was great. But then Mum
had to spoil it by making him write
her a letter too.

Henry hated writing letters for nice
presents every bit as much as he
hated writing them for horrible ones.

"You have to write thank you
letters," said Dad.

"But **why?**" said Henry.

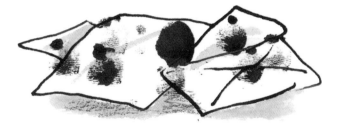

"Because it's polite," said Dad.

"Because people have spent time
and money on you," said Mum.

So what? thought Horrid Henry.
Grown-ups had loads of time to do
whatever they wanted.

No one told them, stop watching
TV and write a thank you letter. Oh
no. They could do it whenever they
felt like it. Or not even do it at all.

And adults had tons of money compared to him. Why shouldn't they spend it buying him presents?

"All you have to do is write
one page," said Dad.
"What's the big deal?"

Henry stared at him. Did Dad have
no idea how long it would take him
to write one whole page?

Hours

and

hours

and

hours.

"You're the meanest, most horrible
parents in the world and I hate you!"
shrieked Horrid Henry.

"Go to your room, Henry!"
shouted Dad.

"And don't come down until
you've written those letters,"
shouted Mum. "I am sick and tired
of arguing about this."

Horrid Henry stomped upstairs.

Chapter 3

Well, no way was Henry writing
any thank you letters.

He'd rather **starve**.

He'd rather **die**.

He'd stay in his room for a month.

A **year**.

One day Mum and Dad would come
up to check on him and all they'd
find would be a few bones.
Then they'd be sorry.

Actually, knowing them, they'd
probably just moan about the mess.
And then Peter would be all happy
because he'd get Henry's room and
Henry's room was bigger.

Well, no way would he give them
the satisfaction.

All right, thought Horrid Henry.
Dad said to write one page. In his
biggest, most gigantic handwriting,
Henry wrote:

DEAR AUNT RUBY,
THANK YOU FOR THE PRESENT.
HENRY

That certainly filled a whole page,
thought Horrid Henry.

Mum came into the room.
"Have you written your letters yet?"

"Yes," lied Henry.

Mum glanced over his shoulder. "Henry!" said Mum. "That is not a proper thank you letter."

"Yes it is," snarled Henry. "Dad said I had to write one page so I wrote one page."

"Write five sentences," said Mum.

Five sentences?

Five whole sentences?

It was completely impossible
for anyone to write so much.
His hand would fall off.

"That's way too much,"
wailed Henry.

"No TV until you write your letters," said Mum, leaving the room.

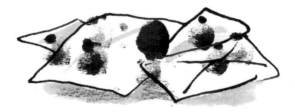

Chapter 4

Horrid Henry stuck out his tongue.
He had the meanest, most horrible
parents in the world.

When he was king any parent
who even whispered the words
'thank you letter' would get fed
to the crocodiles.

They wanted five sentences?
He'd give them five sentences.

Henry picked up his pencil
and scrawled:

Dear Aunt Ruby,
No thank you for the
horrible present. It is
the worst present I have
ever had.

Anyway, didn't some old
Roman say it was better to
give than to receive? So in
fact, you should be writing
me a thank you letter.
    Henry
P.S. Next time just
send money.

There! Five whole sentences.
Perfect, thought Horrid Henry.

Mum said he had to write a five
sentence thank you letter. She never
said it had to be a *nice* thank you
letter. Suddenly Henry felt quite
cheerful.

He folded the letter and popped
it in the stamped envelope Mum
had given him.

One down. Two to go.

In fact, Aunt Ruby's no thank you
letter would do just fine for
Great-Aunt Greta.
He'd just substitute
Great-Aunt Greta's name for
Aunt Ruby's and copy the rest.

Bingo. Another letter was done.

Now Grandma. She *had* sent money so he'd have to write something nice.

> Thank you for the money, blah, blah, blah, best present I've ever received, blah, blah, blah, next year send more money, £15 isn't very much, Ralph got £20 from his grandma, blah, blah, blah.

What a waste, thought Horrid Henry
as he signed it and put it in the
envelope, to spend so much time on a
letter, only to have to write the same
old thing all over again next year.

And then suddenly
Horrid Henry had a wonderful,
spectacular idea.

Why had he never thought of
this before?

He would be

rich,

rich,

rich.

"There goes money-bags Henry,"
kids would whisper enviously, as he
swaggered down the street followed
by Peter lugging a hundred DVDs for
Henry to watch in his mansion on
one of his twenty-eight giant TVs.

Mum and Dad and Peter would be
living in their hovel somewhere,
and if they were very, very nice
to him Henry *might* let them watch
one of his smaller TVs for fifteen
minutes or so once a month.

Henry was going to start a business.
A business guaranteed to make
him rich.

Chapter 5

"Step right up, step right up,"
said Horrid Henry.

He was wearing a sign saying:

HENRy's Thank you letters
personal letters Written
just for you

A small crowd of children
gathered round him.

"I'll write all your thank you letters
for you," said Henry. "All you
have to do is to give me a stamped,
addressed envelope and tell me what
present you got. I'll do the rest."

"How much for a thank you letter?"
asked Kung-Fu Kate.

"£1," said Henry.

"No way," said
Greedy Graham.

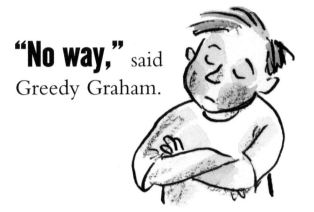

"99p," said Henry.

"Forget it," said
Lazy Linda.

"OK, 50p," said Henry.
"And two for 75p."

"Done," said Linda.

Henry opened his notebook.
"And what were the presents?" he asked.

Linda made a face.
"Handkerchiefs," she spat.
"And a bookmark."

"I can do a 'no thank you' letter,"
said Henry.
"I'm very good at those."

Linda considered.

"Tempting," she said, "but then
mean Uncle John won't send
something better next time."

Business was brisk.
Dave bought three. Ralph bought
four 'no thank you's'.
Even Moody Margaret bought one.

Whoopee, thought Horrid Henry.

His pockets were jingle-jangling
with cash.

Now all he had to do was write seventeen letters. Henry tried not to think about that.

Chapter 6

The moment he got home
from school Henry went
straight to his room.
Right, to work, thought Henry.

His heart sank as he looked at the
blank pages. All those letters!
He would be here for weeks.
Why had he ever set up a
letter-writing business?

But then Horrid Henry thought.

True, he'd promised a personal letter
but how would Linda's aunt ever
find out that Margaret's granny had
received the same one?
She wouldn't!

If he used the computer, it would be
a cinch. And it would be a letter sent
personally, thought Henry, because
I am a person and I will personally
print it out and send it.

All he'd have to do was to write the
names at the top and to sign them.

Easy-peasy lemon squeezy.

Then again, all that signing.
And writing all those names at the
top. And separating the thank you
letters from the no thank you ones.

Maybe there was a better way.

Horrid Henry sat down at the computer and typed:

> **Dear Sir or Madam,**

That should cover everyone, thought Henry, and I won't have to write anyone's name.

> **Thank you/No thank you**
>
> **for the**
>
> **a) wonderful**
>
> **b) horrible**
>
> **c) disgusting**
>
> **present.**

70

I really loved/hated it.

In fact, it is the best present/worst

present I have ever received.

I played with it/broke it/ate it/spent it/

threw it in the bin straight away.

Next time just send lots of money.

Best wishes/ worst wishes,

Now, how to sign it?
Aha, thought Henry.

Your friend

or relative.

Perfect, thought Horrid Henry.
Sir or Madam knows whether
they deserve a thank you
or a no thank you letter.
Let them do some work for a change
and tick the correct answers.

Print.

Print.

Print.

Out spewed seventeen letters.

It only took a moment to stuff
the letters in the envelopes.
He'd pop them in the postbox
on the way to school.
Had an easier way to become a
millionaire ever been invented?
thought Horrid Henry, as he turned
on the telly.

Ding dong.

It was two weeks after Henry set up
'Henry's Thank You Letters'.
Horrid Henry opened the door.
A group of Henry's customers
stood there, waving pieces of paper
and shouting.

"My granny sent the letter back and now I can't watch TV for a week," wailed Moody Margaret.

"I'm grounded!"
screamed Aerobic Al.

"I have to go swimming!"
screamed Lazy Linda.

"No sweets!"
yelped Greedy Graham.

"No pocket money!"
screamed Rude Ralph.

"And it's all
your fault!"
they shouted.

Horrid Henry glared at his angry
customers. He was outraged.
After all his hard work, *this* was
the thanks he got?

"Too bad!" said Horrid Henry as he
slammed the door. Honestly, there
was no pleasing some people.

"Henry," said Mum.
"I just had the strangest phone call
from Aunt Ruby…"

HORRiD HENRY
Meets the Queen

Contents

For Mary Clayton and
Niall MacMonagle

Chapter 1

Perfect Peter bowed to himself
in the mirror.

"Your Majesty," he said,
pretending to present a bouquet.

"Welcome to our school,
your Majesty.
My name is Peter, your Majesty.
Thank you, your Majesty.
Goodbye, your Majesty."

Slowly Perfect Peter retreated
backwards, bowing and smiling.

"Oh shut up," snarled Horrid Henry.
He glared at Peter.

If Peter said "Your Majesty" one
more time, he would, he would…
Horrid Henry wasn't sure what
he'd do, but it would be horrible.

The Queen was coming to
Henry's school!

The real live Queen!

The real live Queen, with her dogs
and jewels and crowns and castles
and beefeaters and knights and horses
and ladies-in-waiting, was coming to
see the Tudor wall they had built.

Yet for some reason Horrid Henry
had not been asked to give the
Queen a bouquet.
Instead, the head, Mrs Oddbod,
had chosen Peter.

Peter!

Why stupid smelly old ugly toad
Peter? It was so unfair.

Chapter 2

Just because Peter had more stars
than anyone in the 'Good as Gold'
book, was that any reason to
choose *him*?

Henry should have been chosen.
He would do a much better job
than Peter. Besides, he wanted to ask
the Queen how many TVs she had.
Now he'd never get the chance.

"Your Majesty," said Peter, bowing.

"Your Majesty,"
mimicked Henry, curtseying.

Perfect Peter ignored him.
He'd been ignoring Henry a lot
ever since *he'd* been chosen to
meet the Queen.

Come to think of it, everyone had
been ignoring Henry.

"Isn't it thrilling?"
said Mum for the millionth time.

"Isn't it fantastic?"
said Dad for the billionth time.

"NO!"

Henry had said.

Chapter 3

Who'd want to hand some rotten
flowers to a stupid queen anyhow?

Not Horrid Henry.

And he certainly didn't want
to have his picture in the paper,
and everyone making a fuss.

"Bow, bouquet, answer her question, walk away," muttered Perfect Peter. Then he paused. "Or is it bouquet, bow?"

Horrid Henry had had just about enough of Peter showing off.

"You're doing it all wrong,"
said Henry.

"No I'm not," said Peter.

"Yes you are," said Henry.
"You're supposed to hold the
bouquet up to her nose, so she can
have a sniff before you give it to her."

Perfect Peter paused.
"No I'm not," said Peter.

Horrid Henry shook his head sadly.
"I think we'd better practise,"
he said. "Pretend I'm the Queen."
He picked up Peter's shiny silver
crown, covered in fool's jewels,
and put it on his head.

Perfect Peter beamed. He'd been begging Henry to practise with him all morning. "Ask me a question the Queen would ask," said Peter.

Horrid Henry considered.
"Why are you so smelly, little boy?"
said the Queen, holding her nose.

"The Queen wouldn't ask *that*!"
gasped Perfect Peter.

"Yes she would," said Henry.

"Wouldn't."

"Would."

"And I'm not smelly!"

Horrid Henry waved his hand
in front of his face.

"Poo!" said the Queen. "Take this
smelly boy to the Tower."

"Stop it, Henry," said Peter.
"Ask me a real question,
like my name or what year I'm in."

"Why are you so ugly?"
said the Queen.

"MUM!" wailed Peter. "Henry called me ugly. And smelly."

"Don't be horrid, Henry!" shouted Mum.

Chapter 4

"Do you want me to practise with you or don't you?" hissed Henry.

"Practise," sniffed Peter.

"Well, go on then," said Henry.

Perfect Peter walked up to Henry and bowed.

"Wrong!" said Henry. "You don't bow to the Queen, you curtsey."

"Curtsey?" said Peter.
Mrs Oddbod hadn't said anything
about curtseying. "But I'm a boy."

"The law was changed," said Henry.
"Everyone curtseys now."

Peter hesitated.
"Are you sure?" asked Peter.

"Yes," said Henry. "And when
you meet the Queen, you put your
thumb on your nose and wriggle
your fingers. Like this."

Horrid Henry cocked a snook.

Perfect Peter gasped.
Mrs Oddbod hadn't said anything
about thumbs on noses.

"But that's … rude,"
said Perfect Peter.

"Not to the Queen," said Horrid
Henry. "You can't just say 'hi'
to the Queen like she's a person.
She's the Queen. There are special
rules. If you get it wrong she can
chop off your head."

Chop off his head!

Mrs Oddbod hadn't said anything about chopping off heads.

"That's not true," said Peter.

"Yes it is," said Henry.

"Isn't!"

Horrid Henry sighed.
"If you get it wrong, you'll be
locked up in the Tower," he said.
"It's high treason to greet the
Queen the wrong way.
Everyone knows that."

Perfect Peter paused. Mrs Oddbod
hadn't said anything about being
locked up in the Tower.

"I don't believe you, Henry,"
said Peter.

Henry shrugged.
"OK. Just don't blame me when you
get your head chopped off."

Come to think of it, thought Peter,
there was a lot of head-chopping
when people met kings and queens.
But surely that was just in the
olden days…

"MUM!" screamed Peter.

Mum ran into the room.

"Henry said I had to curtsey
to the Queen," wailed Peter.
"And that I'd get my head chopped
off if I got it wrong."

Mum glared at Henry.
"How *could* you be so horrid, Henry?
said Mum. "Go to your room!"

"Fine!" screeched Horrid Henry.

"I'll practise with you, Peter,"
said Mum.

"Bow, bouquet, answer her question,
walk away," said Peter, beaming.

Chapter 5

The great day arrived.
The entire school lined up in the
playground, waiting for the Queen.

Perfect Peter, dressed in his best
party clothes, stood with Mrs
Oddbod by the gate.
A large black car pulled up
in front of the school.

"There she is!" shrieked the children.

Horrid Henry was furious.
Miss Battle-Axe had made him stand
in the very last row, as far away from
the Queen as he could be.

How on earth could he find out
if she had 300 TVs standing way
back here?

Anyone would think Miss Battle-Axe
wanted to keep him away from the
Queen on purpose, thought Henry,
scowling.

Perfect Peter waited, clutching
an enormous bouquet of flowers.
His big moment was here.

"Bow, bouquet, answer her
question, walk away. Bow, bouquet,
answer her question, walk away,"
mumbled Peter.

"Don't worry, Peter, you'll be
perfect," whispered Mrs Oddbod,
urging him forward.

Horrid Henry pushed and shoved
to get a closer view.

Yes, there was his stupid brother,
looking like a worm.

Perfect Peter walked slowly
towards the Queen.
"Bow, bouquet, answer her question,
walk away," he mumbled.

Suddenly that didn't sound right.
Was it bow, bouquet?
Or bouquet, bow?

The Queen looked down at Peter.

Peter looked up at the Queen.

"Your Majesty," he said.
Now what was he supposed
to do next?

Chapter 6

Peter's heart began to pound.
His mind was blank.

Peter bowed.
The bouquet smacked him
in the face.

"Owww!" yelped Peter.

What had he practised?
Ah yes, now he remembered!
Peter curtseyed.
Then he cocked a snook.

Mrs Oddbod gasped.

Oh no, what had he done wrong?

Aaarrgh, the bouquet!
It was still in his hand.
Quickly Peter thrust it at the Queen.

Smack!

The flowers hit her in the face.

"How lovely," said the Queen.

"Waaaa!" wailed Peter.
"Don't chop off my head!"

There was a very long silence.
Henry saw his chance.

"How many TVs have you got?"
shouted Horrid Henry.

The Queen did not seem
to have heard.

"Come along everyone, to the
display of Tudor daub-making,"
said Mrs Oddbod.
She looked a little pale.

"I said," shouted Henry.
"How many…"

A long, bony arm yanked him away.

"Be quiet, Henry,"
hissed Miss Battle-Axe.
"Go to the back playground like
we practised. I don't want to hear
another word out of you."

Horrid Henry trudged off to the
vat of daub with Miss Battle-Axe's
beady eyes watching his every step.
It was so unfair!

When everyone was in their assigned
place, Mrs Oddbod spoke.
"Your Majesty, mums and dads, boys
and girls, the Tudors used mud and
straw to make daub for their walls.
Miss Battle-Axe's class will now
show you how."

She nodded to the children standing
in the vat. The school recorder band
played *Greensleeves*.

Henry's class began to stomp in the
vat of mud and straw.

"How lovely," said the Queen.

Horrid Henry stomped where
he'd been placed between Jazzy Jim
and Aerobic Al.

There was a whole vat of stomping
children blocking him from the
Queen, who was seated
in the front row between
Miss Battle-Axe and Mrs Oddbod.

If only he could get closer to the
Queen. Then he could find out
about those TVs! Henry noticed a
tiny space between Brainy Brian
and Gorgeous Gurinder.
Henry stomped his way through it.

"Hey!" said Brian.

"Oww!" said Gurinder.
"That was my foot!"

Henry ignored them.

Chapter 7

Stomp.
Stomp.
Stomp.

Henry pounded past
Greedy Graham and Weepy William.

"Oy!" said Graham. "Stop pushing."

"Waaaaaaa!" wept Weepy William.

Halfway to the front!
Henry pushed past Anxious Andrew
and Clever Clare.

"Hellllppp!"
squeaked Andrew, falling over.

"Watch out, Henry," snapped Clare.

Almost there!
Just Moody Margaret and Jolly Josh
stood in his way.

Margaret stomped.

Josh stomped.

Henry trampled through the daub
till he stood right behind Margaret.

Squish.

Squash.

Squish.

Squash.

"Stop stomping on my bit,"
hissed Moody Margaret.

"Stop stomping on my bit,"
said Horrid Henry.

"I was here first," said Margaret.

"No you weren't," said Henry.
"Now get out of my way."

"Make me," said Moody Margaret.

Henry stomped harder.

Squelch! Squelch! Squelch!

Margaret stomped harder.

Stomp! Stomp! Stomp!

Rude Ralph pushed forward.
So did Dizzy Dave.

Stomp!

Stomp!

Stomp!

Sour Susan pushed forward.
So did Kung-Fu Kate.

Stomp!

Stomp!

Stomp!

Stomp!

Stomp!

A tidal wave of mud and straw
flew out of the vat.

 # Splat!

Miss Battle-Axe was covered.

Splat!

Mrs Oddbod was covered.

Splat!

The Queen was covered.

"Oops," said Horrid Henry.

Mrs Oddbod fainted.

"How lovely,"
mumbled the Queen.

MOODY MARGARET'S
School

Contents

To Sue Michniewicz,
for all her lovely work on Horrid Henry

Chapter 1

"Pay attention, Susan,"
shrieked Moody Margaret,
"or you'll go straight to the head."

"I *am* paying attention,"
said Sour Susan.

"This is boring,"
said Horrid Henry.
"I want to play pirates."

"Silence," said Moody Margaret, whacking her ruler on the table.

"I want to be the teacher,"
said Susan.

"No," said Margaret.

"*I'll* be the teacher," said Horrid
Henry. He'd send the class straight
out for playtime, and tell them
to run for their lives.

"Are you out of your mind?"
snapped Margaret.

"Can I be the teacher?"
asked Perfect Peter.

"NO!" shouted Margaret,
Susan, and Henry.

"Why can't I be the head?"
said Susan sourly.

"Because," said Margaret.

"'Cause why?" said Susan.

"'Cause *I'm* the head."

"But you're the head *and* the teacher," said Susan. "It's not fair."

"It is too fair, 'cause you'd make a terrible head," said Margaret.

"Wouldn't!"

"Would!"

"I think we should take turns
being head," said Susan.

"That," said Margaret, "is the
dumbest idea I've ever heard.
Do you see Mrs Oddbod taking *turns*
being head? I don't think so."

Margaret's class grumbled
mutinously on the carpet inside
the Secret Club tent.

Chapter 2

"Class, I will now take
the register," intoned Margaret.

"Susan?"

Here.

"Peter?"

Here.

"Henry?"

"In the toilet."

Margaret scowled.
"We'll try that again. Henry?"

"Flushed away."

"Last chance,"
said Margaret severely. "Henry?"

"Dead."

Margaret made a big cross in
her register.
"I will deal with you later."

"No one made *you* the big boss,"
muttered Horrid Henry.

"It's *my* house and we'll play what
I want," said Moody Margaret.
"And I want to play school."

Horrid Henry scowled.

Whenever Margaret came to
his house she was the guest and
he had to play what *she* wanted.
But whenever Henry went to
her house Margaret was the boss
'cause it was *her* house.

Ugggh.

Why oh why did he have to live
next door to Moody Margaret?

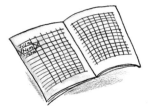

Chapter 3

Mum had important work to do,
and needed total peace and quiet,
so Henry and Peter had been
dumped at Margaret's.

Henry had begged to go
to Ralph's, but Ralph was visiting
his grandparents.

Now he was trapped all day with
a horrible, moody old grouch.

Wasn't it bad enough being with
Miss Battle-Axe all week without
having to spend his whole precious
Saturday stuck at Margaret's?
And, even worse, playing school?

"Come on, let's play pirates,"
said Henry.
"I'm Captain Hook.
Peter, walk the plank!"

"No," said Margaret.
"I don't want to."

"But I'm the guest,"
protested Henry.

"So?" said Margaret.
"This is *my* house and
we play by *my* rules."

"Yeah, Henry," said Sour Susan.

"And I love playing school,"
said Perfect Peter.
"It's such fun doing sums."

Grrr.

If only Henry could just go home.

"I want a good report," Mum had
said, "or you won't be going to
Dave's bowling party tonight. It's
very kind of Margaret and her mum
to have you boys over to play."

"But I don't want to go to
Margaret's!" howled Henry. "I want
to stay home and watch TV!"

"N-O spells no,"

said Mum, and sent him kicking
and screaming next door. "You can
come home at five o'clock to get
ready for Dave's party and not a
minute before."

Horrid Henry gazed longingly
over the wall.

His house looked so inviting.
There was his bedroom window,
twinkling at him.

And his lonesome telly, stuck all by
itself in the sitting room, just begging
him to come over and switch it on.

And all his wonderful toys, just
waiting to be played with.

Funny, thought Horrid Henry,
his toys seemed so boring when he
was in his room. But now that he
was trapped at Margaret's, there was
so much he longed to do at home.

Wait.

He could hide out in his fort
until five. Yes!
Then he'd stroll into his house as
if he'd been at Margaret's all day.

But then Margaret's mum would
be sure to call his mum to say that
Henry had vanished and Henry
would get into trouble.

Big, big
trouble.
Big, big,
banned from
Dave's party trouble.

Or, he'd pretend to be sick.
Margaret's mum was such an
old fusspot she'd be sure to send
him home immediately.

Yippee.

He was a genius. This would be easy.

A few loud coughs, a few dramatic
clutches at his stomach, a dash to the
loo, and he'd be sent straight home
and …

Oops. He'd be put to bed.

No party.

No pizza.

No bowling.

And what was the point of
pretending to be sick at the *weekend*?
He was trapped.

Chapter 4

Moody Margaret whacked her ruler
on the table.

"I want everyone to write
a story," said Margaret.

Write a story!
Boy would Horrid Henry write
a story. He seized a piece of paper
and a pencil and scribbled away.

"Who'd like to read their story to the class?" said Margaret.

"I will," said Henry.

Once upon a time there was a moody old grouch named Margaret.

Margaret had been born a frog but an ugly wizard cursed the frog and turned it into Margaret.

"That's enough, Henry,"
snapped Margaret.

Henry ignored her.

"Ribbet ribbet,"
said Margaret Frog.
"Ribbet ribbet ribbet."
Everyone in the kingdom
tried to get rid of this
horrible croaking moody
monster. But she smelled
so awful that no one could
get near her.

And then one day a hero
named Heroic Henry came,
and he held his nose, grabbed
the Margaret Monster and
hurled her into outer space
where she exploded and was
never seen again.

THE END

Susan giggled.

Margaret glared.

"Fail," said Margaret.

"Why?" said Horrid Henry
innocently.

"'Cause," said Margaret. "I'm the
teacher and I say it was boring."

"Did you think my story was boring,
Peter?" demanded Henry.

Peter looked nervous.

"Did you?" said Margaret.

"Well, uhm, uhmm, I think mine
is better," said Peter.

Once upon a time there was
a tea towel named Terry.
He was a very sad tea towel
because he didn't have any
dishes to dry. One day he
found a lot of wet dishes.
Swish swish swish, they were
dry in no time. "Yippee,"
said Terry the Tea Towel,
"I wonder when —"

"Boring!" shouted Horrid Henry.

"Excellent, Peter,"
said Moody Margaret.
"*Much* better than Henry's."

Susan read out a story about her cat.

My cat Kitty Kat is a big fat cat.

She says meow.

One day Kitty Kat met a dog.

Meow, said Kitty Kat.

Woof woof, said the dog.

Kitty Kat ran away.

So did the dog.

The end.

"OK, class, here are your marks,"
said Margaret. "Peter came first."

"Yay!" said Perfect Peter.

"*What?*" said Susan.
"My story was way better than his."

"Susan came second,
Henry came ninth."

"How can I be ninth if there are only three people in the class?" demanded Horrid Henry.

"'Cause that's how bad your story was," said Margaret. "Now, I've done some worksheets for you. No talking or there'll be no break."

"Goody," said Perfect Peter.
"I love worksheets. Are there lots
of hard spelling words to learn?

Chapter 5

Horrid Henry had had enough.
It was time to turn into
Heroic Henry and destroy this
horrible hag.

Henry crumpled up his worksheet
and stood up.
"I've just been pretending to
be a student," shouted Henry.
"In fact, I'm a school inspector.
And I'm shutting your school down.
It's a disgrace."

Margaret gasped.

"You're a moody old grouch
and a terrible teacher,"
said the inspector.

"I am not," said Margaret.

"She is not," said Susan.

"Silence when the inspector
is speaking! You're the worst teacher
I've ever seen. Imagine marking
a stupid story about a tea towel
higher than a fantastic tale about
a wicked wizard."

"I'm the head," said Margaret.
"You can't boss me around."

"I'm the inspector," said Henry.
"I can boss *everyone* around."

"Wrong, Henry," said Margaret,
"because I'm the *chief* school
inspector, and I'm inspecting *you*."

"Oh no you're not,"

said Henry.

"Oh yes I am,"

said Margaret.

"An inspector can't be a head
and a teacher, so there,"
said Henry.

"Oh yes I can,"

said Margaret.

"No you can't, 'cause I'm king and I send you to the Tower!" shrieked King Henry the Horrible.

"I'm the empress!" screamed Margaret. "Go to jail."

"I'm king of the universe,
and I send you to the snakepit,"
shrieked Henry.

"I'm queen of the universe and I'm
going to chop off your head!"

"Not if I chop off yours first!"
shrieked the king, yanking
on the queen's hair.

The queen screamed
and kicked the king.

The king screamed
and kicked the queen.

"MUM!" screamed Margaret.

Chapter 6

Margaret's mother rushed into
the Secret Club tent.

"What's wrong with my little snugglechops?" said Margaret's mum.

"Henry's not playing my game," said Margaret. "And he kicked me."

"She kicked me first," said Henry.

"If you children can't play nicely
I'll have to send you all home,"
said Margaret's mother severely.

"No!" said Peter.

Send him … home.

Yes!

Henry would make Margaret scream
until the walls fell down.
He would tell Margaret's mum
her house smelled of poo.
He could ... he would ...

But if Henry was sent home for
being horrid, Mum and Dad would
be furious. There'd be no pizza and
bowling party for sure.

Unless … unless … It was risky.
It was dangerous. It could go
horribly, horribly wrong.
But desperate times call for
desperate measures.

"Need a drink," said Henry,
and ran out of the tent before
Margaret could stop him.

Henry went into the kitchen
to find Margaret's mum.

"I'm worried about Margaret, I think she's getting sick," said Henry.

"My little Maggie-muffin?" gasped Margaret's mum.

"She's being very strange," said Henry sadly. "She said she's the queen of the world and she would cut off my head."

"Margaret would *never* say such
a thing," said her mum. "She always
plays beautifully. I've never seen
a child so good at sharing."

Horrid Henry nodded.
"I know. It must be 'cause she's sick.
Maybe she caught something
from Peter."

"Has Peter been ill?" said Margaret's mum. She looked pale.

"Oh yeah," lied Henry. "He's been throwing up, and – and – well, it's been awful. But I'm sure he's not *very* contagious."

"Throwing up?"
said Margaret's mum weakly.

"And diarrhoea," said Henry.
"Loads and loads."

Margaret's mother looked ashen.
"Diarrhoea?"

"But he's much better now," said
Henry. "He's only run to the loo
five times since we've been here."

Margaret's mother looked faint.
"My little Margaret is so delicate …
I can't risk …" she gasped. "I think
you and Peter had better go home
straight away. Margaret! Margaret!
Come in at once," she shouted.

Horrid Henry did not wait to be
told twice. School was out!

Ahhhh, thought Horrid Henry
happily, reaching for the TV clicker,
this was the life.

Margaret had been sent to bed.
He and Peter had been sent home.

There was enough time to watch
Marvin the Maniac and *Terminator
Gladiator* before Dave's party.

"I can't help it that Margaret
wasn't feeling well, Mum,"
said Horrid Henry.
"I just hope I haven't caught
anything from *her*."

Honestly.
Mum was so selfish.

HORRID HENRY'S
Sports Day

Contents

For Max and Zoë Cutner,
always first past the post.

Chapter 1

"We all want Sports Day to be a great success tomorrow," announced Miss Battle-Axe. "I am here to make sure that *no one*" – she glared at Horrid Henry – "spoils it."

Horrid Henry glared back.
Horrid Henry hated Sports Day.
Last year he hadn't won a
single event.

He'd dropped his egg in the
egg-and-spoon race,

tripped over Rude Ralph in the
three-legged race,

and collided with Sour Susan
in the sack race.

Henry's team had even lost
the tug-of-war.

Most sickening of all, Perfect Peter
had won both his races.

If only the school had a sensible day,
like TV-watching day, or chocolate-
eating day, or who could guzzle the
most crisps day, Horrid Henry would
be sure to win every prize.

But no. *He* had to leap and dash about getting hot and bothered in front of stupid parents.

When he became king he'd make teachers run all the races then behead the winners. King Henry the Horrible grinned happily.

"Pay attention, Henry!" barked Miss
Battle-Axe. "What did I just say?"

Henry had no idea.
"Sports Day is cancelled?"
he suggested hopefully.

Miss Battle-Axe fixed him with
her steely eyes. "I said no one is to
bring any sweets tomorrow.
You'll all be given a delicious,
refreshing piece of orange."

Henry slumped in his chair,
scowling. All he could do was
hope for rain.

Chapter 2

Sports Day dawned bright and sunny.

Rats, thought Henry.
He could, of course, pretend to
be sick. But he'd tried that last year
and Mum hadn't been fooled.

The year before that he'd
complained he'd hurt his leg.
Unfortunately Dad then caught
him dancing on the table.

It was no use. He'd just have to take
part. If only he could win a race!

Perfect Peter bounced into his room.
"Sports Day today!" beamed Peter.
"And *I'm* responsible for bringing
the hard-boiled eggs for the egg-and-
spoon race. Isn't it exciting!"

"NO!" screeched Henry.
"Get out of here!"

"But I only..." began Peter.

Henry leapt at him, roaring. He was
a cowboy lassoing a runaway steer.
"Eeeaaargh!" squealed Peter.

"Stop being horrid, Henry!"
shouted Dad.
"Or no pocket money this week!"
Henry let Peter go.

"It's so unfair," he muttered, picking up his clothes from the floor and putting them on.
Why did he never win?

Chapter 3

Henry reached under his bed and
filled his pockets from the secret
sweet tin he kept there.

Horrid Henry was a master at eating sweets in school without being detected. At least he could scoff something good while the others were stuck eating dried-up old orange pieces.

Then he stomped downstairs.

Perfect Peter was busy packing
hard-boiled eggs into a carton.
Horrid Henry sat down scowling
and gobbled his breakfast.

"Good luck, boys," said Mum.
"I'll be there to cheer for you."

"Humph," growled Henry.

"Thanks, Mum," said Peter.
"I expect I'll win my egg-and-spoon
race again but of course it doesn't
matter if I don't. It's how you play
that counts."

"Shut up, Peter!" snarled Henry.

Egg-and-spoon!

Egg-and-spoon!

If Henry heard that disgusting phrase
once more he would start frothing
at the mouth.

"Mum! Henry told me to shut up,"
wailed Peter, "and he attacked me
this morning."

"Stop being horrid, Henry,"
said Mum. "Peter, come with me
and we'll comb your hair. I want
you to look your best when you
win that trophy again."

Henry's blood boiled. He felt like
snatching those eggs and hurling
them against the wall.

Then Henry had a wonderful,
spectacular idea. It was so
wonderful that… Henry heard Mum
coming back down the stairs.
There was no time to lose crowing
about his brilliance.

Horrid Henry ran to the fridge,
grabbed another egg carton and
swapped it for the box of hard-boiled
ones on the counter.

"Don't forget your eggs, Peter," said Mum. She handed the carton to Peter, who tucked it safely in his school bag.

Tee hee, thought Horrid Henry.

Chapter 4

Henry's class lined up on the
playing fields.

Flash!

A small figure wearing gleaming
white trainers zipped by.
It was Aerobic Al, the fastest boy
in Henry's class.

"Gotta run, gotta run, gotta run,"
he chanted, gliding into place beside
Henry. "I will, of course, win every
event," he announced.
"I've been training all year.
My dad's got a special place all ready
for my trophies."

"Who wants to race anyway?"
sneered Horrid Henry, sneaking
a yummy gummy fuzzball into
his mouth.

"Now, teams for the three-legged race," barked Miss Battle-Axe into her megaphone. "This is a race showing how well you co-operate and use teamwork with your partner.

Ralph will race with William,

Josh will race with Clare,

Henry…" She glanced at her list.
"You will race with Margaret."

"NO!"

screamed Horrid Henry.

"NO!"

screamed Moody Margaret.

"Yes," said Miss Battle-Axe.

"But I want to be with Susan,"
said Margaret.

"No fussing," said Miss Battle-Axe.
"Bert, where's your partner?"

"I dunno," said Beefy Bert.

Henry and Margaret stood as far
apart as possible while their legs
were tied together.

"You'd better do as I say, Henry,"
hissed Margaret.
"*I'll* decide how we race."

"*I* will, you mean," hissed Henry.

"Ready … steady …GO!"
Miss Battle-Axe blew her whistle.
They were off!

Chapter 5

Henry moved to the left,
Margaret moved to the right.

"This way, Henry!" shouted
Margaret. She tried to drag him.

"No, this way!" shouted Henry.
He tried to drag her.

They lurched wildly, left and right,
then toppled over.

CRASH!

Aerobic Al and Lazy Linda
tripped over the screaming Henry
and Margaret.

SMASH!

Rude Ralph and Weepy William
fell over Al and Linda.

BUMP!

Dizzy Dave and Beefy Bert collided
with Ralph and William.

"Waaa!"

wailed Weepy William.

"It's all your fault, Margaret!"
shouted Henry, pulling her hair.

"No, yours," shouted Margaret,
pulling his harder.

Miss Battle-Axe blew her whistle
frantically.

"Stop! Stop!" she ordered.
"Henry! Margaret! What an example
to set for the younger ones.
Any more nonsense like that and
you'll be severely punished.

Everyone, get ready for the
egg-and-spoon race!"

This was it!
The moment Henry had been
waiting for.

The children lined up in their teams.
Moody Margaret, Sour Susan and
Anxious Andrew were going first
in Henry's class.

Henry glanced at Peter.
Yes, there he was, smiling proudly,
next to Goody-Goody Gordon,
Spotless Sam, and Tidy Ted.
The eggs lay still on their spoons.

Horrid Henry held his breath.

"Ready ... steady ... GO!"
shouted Miss Battle-Axe.

They were off!

Chapter 6

"Go, Peter, go!" shouted Mum.

Peter walked faster
and faster and faster.

He was in the lead.
He was pulling away from the field.

Then ...

w_obble · · ·

w_obble · · ·

SPLAT!

"Aaaaagh!" yelped Peter.

Moody Margaret's egg wobbled.

SPLAT!

Then Susan's.

SPLAT!

Then everybody's.

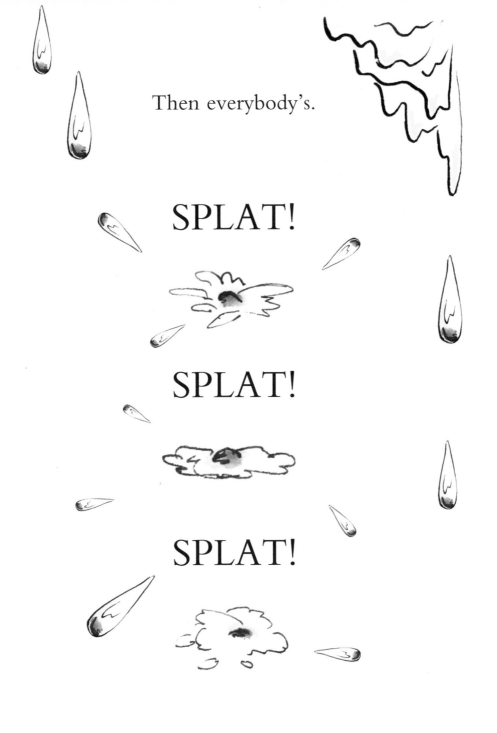

SPLAT!

SPLAT!

SPLAT!

273

"I've got egg on my shoes!"
wailed Margaret.

"I've ruined my new dress!"
shrieked Susan.

"I've got egg all over me!"
squealed Tidy Ted.

"Help!" squeaked Perfect Peter.
Egg dripped down his trousers.

Parents surged forward,
screaming and waving
handkerchiefs and towels.

Rude Ralph and Horrid Henry
shrieked with laughter.

Miss Battle-Axe blew her whistle.
"Who brought the eggs?" asked Miss
Battle-Axe. Her voice was like ice.

"I did," said Perfect Peter.
"But I brought hard-boiled ones."

"OUT!" shouted Miss Battle-Axe.
"Out of the games!"

"But … but …" gasped
Perfect Peter.

"No buts, out!" she glared.
"Go straight to the Head."

Perfect Peter burst into tears
and crept away.

Horrid Henry could hardly contain himself. This was the best Sports Day he'd ever been to.

"The rest of you stop laughing at once. Parents, get back to your seats! Time for the next race!" ordered Miss Battle-Axe.

Chapter 7

All things considered, thought
Horrid Henry, lining up with
his class, it hadn't been too
terrible a day.

He'd loved the egg-and-spoon race,
of course. And he'd had fun pulling
the other team into a muddy puddle
in the tug-of-war, knocking over
the obstacles in the obstacle race,
and crashing into Aerobic Al in
the sack race.

But, oh, to actually win something!

There was just one race left before Sports Day was over. The cross-country run. The event Henry hated more than any other. One long, sweaty, exhausting lap round the whole field.

Henry heaved his heavy bones to the
starting line. His final chance to win
… yet he knew there was no hope.
If he beat Weepy William
he'd be doing well.

Suddenly Henry had a wonderful,
spectacular idea. Why had he never
thought of this before?
Truly, he was a genius.

Wasn't there some ancient Greek who'd won a race by throwing down golden apples which his rival kept stopping to pick up?

Couldn't he, Henry, learn something from those old Greeks?

"Ready …steady … GO!"
shrieked Miss Battle-Axe.

Off they dashed.

"Go, Al, go!" yelled his father.

"Do your best, Henry," said Mum.

Horrid Henry reached into his
pocket and hurled some sweets.
They thudded to the ground
in front of the runners.

"Look, sweets!" shouted Henry.

Al checked behind him.
He was well in the lead. He paused
and scooped up one sweet, and then
another. He glanced behind again,
then started unwrapping the yummy
gummy fuzzball.

"Sweets!" yelped Greedy Graham.
He stopped to pick up as many
as he could find then stuffed them
in his mouth.
"Yummy!" screamed Graham.

"Sweets! Where?" chanted the
others. Then they stopped to look.

"Over there!" yelled Henry,
throwing another handful.

The racers paused to pounce
on the treats.

While the others munched and
crunched, Henry made a frantic dash
for the lead.

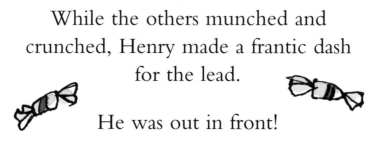

He was out in front!

Henry's legs moved as they had
never moved before, pounding
round the field. And there was
the finishing line!

 THUD!

THUD!

THUD!

Henry glanced back.
Oh no! Aerobic Al was catching up!

Henry felt in his pocket. He had one giant gob-stopper left. He looked round, panting.

"Go home and take a nap, Henry!" shouted Al, sticking out his tongue as he raced past.

Henry threw down the gob-stopper in front of Al. Aerobic Al hesitated, then skidded to a halt and picked it up. He could beat Henry any day so why not show off a bit?

Suddenly Henry sprinted past.
Aerobic Al dashed after him.
Harder and harder, faster and faster
Henry ran. He was a bird.
He was a plane.
He flew across the finishing line.

"The winner is … Henry?"
squeaked Miss Battle-Axe.

"I've been robbed!"
screamed Aerobic Al.

"Hurray!" yelled Henry.

Wow, what a great day, thought
Horrid Henry, proudly carrying
home his trophy. Al's dad shouting
at Miss Battle-Axe. Miss Battle-Axe
and Mum shouting back.
Peter sent off in disgrace.
And he, Henry, the big winner.

"I can't think how you got those eggs muddled up," said Mum.

"Me neither," said Perfect Peter, sniffling.

"Never mind, Peter," said Henry brightly. "It's not winning, it's *how* you play that counts."

What are you going to read next?

More adventures with Horrid Henry,

or go exploring with Shumba,

and brave the Jungle

and Arctic with Algy.

Find a frog prince with Tulsa

or even a big, yellow, whiskery

Lion in the Meadow!

Tuck into some

Blood and Guts and
Rats' Tail Pizza,

learn to dance with
Sophie,

travel back
in time with

Cudweed

and sail away in

Noah's Ark.

Enjoy all the Early Readers.

HORRID HENRY BOOKS

Visit Horrid Henry's website at **www.horridhenry.co.uk**
for competitions, games, downloads and a monthly newsletter.

the orion star

Sign up for **the orion star** newsletter
for all the latest children's book news,
plus activity sheets, exclusive competitions,
author interviews, pre-publication extracts
and more.

www.orionbooks.co.uk/newsletters

Follow @the_orionstar on twitter.

Orion
Children's Books